Making Decisions on the Supreme Court

UNDERSTANDING GOVERNMENT

Leona Fowler

CIVICS FOR THE REAL WORLD™

Rosen Classroom™

Published in 2019 by The Rosen Publishing Group, Inc.
29 East 21st Street, New York, NY 10010

Book Design: Haley Robinson
Editor: Ryan Wolf

Photo Credits: Cover Orhan Cam/Shutterstock.com; p. 4 Konstantin L/Shutterstock.com; p. 7 Rob Crandall/Shutterstock.com; p. 8 Alex Staroseltsev/Shutterstock.com; p. 11 Mike Flippo/Shutterstock.com; p. 12 wavebreakmedia/Shutterstock.com; p. 14 https://commons.wikimedia.org/wiki/File:Supreme_Court_of_the_United_States_-_Roberts_Court_2017.jpg.

ISBN: 9781538365199
6-pack ISBN: 9781538365205

Manufactured in the United States of America

CPSIA Compliance Information: Batch #WS18RC: For Further Information contact Rosen Publishing, New York, New York at 1-800-237-9932

Table of Contents

The Highest Court

The **Supreme** Court is the most powerful court in the United States. It's the only court created and named in the U.S. **Constitution**. The Supreme Court decides many law cases every year. It has a very important job in the U.S. government! These cases may affect many people's lives.

Who Decides?

The members of the Supreme Court are called justices. There is one chief justice and eight **associate** justices. The president of the United States picks a new justice when there is an open spot. Justices have usually worked as **lawyers** and judges. The Senate must approve them. The Senate is part of Congress, the group that makes U.S. laws.

Cases for the Court

Sometimes the Supreme Court deals with cases between two states. Most of the time, though, it handles appeals. This is when people ask a higher court to reconsider the decision of a lower court. The Supreme Court is the highest court. It's the last stop a case can make!

Hard Choices

The justices of the Supreme Court must pick the appeals they'll hear. They don't hear every appeal they get. In fact, they only take fewer than one of every ten appeals. Supreme Court cases must have something to do with **federal** law or the Constitution. The justices only take the hardest cases.

U.S. Constitution

Hearing the Case

In a Supreme Court appeal, lawyers for both sides get to stand in front of the justices. They tell them what they think. The justices listen. Then they question the lawyers. They ask a lot of hard questions! Then they go into a room to talk and vote on a decision.

Agreeing and Disagreeing

More than half the justices must agree on each decision. Once the court decides, only another Supreme Court decision or a change to the Constitution can undo that decision. The Supreme Court can also undo laws if it decides they go against the U.S. Constitution. It's a very important part of our government!

Glossary

associate: Having a lower status in an organization.

constitution: The basic laws by which a country, state, or group is governed.

federal: Relating to the central government of the United States.

lawyer: Someone whose job it is to help people with their questions and problems with the law.

supreme: The highest in rank or power.

Index